Shine

Lily's Secret Audition

For all my family – HW

To Felix, my son, I will always believe in you and
your dreams! – MD

~

First American Edition 2020
Kane Miller, A Division of EDC Publishing

Originally published in Great Britain under the title *Lily Under Pressure*
by Bloomsbury Publishing Plc in 2007. Published in Great Britain in
2019 by STRIPES Publishing, an imprint of the Little Tiger Group.
Text copyright © Holly Webb, 2007, 2019
Illustrations copyright © Monique Dong, 2019
The moral rights of the author and illustrator have been asserted.

For information contact:
Kane Miller, A Division of EDC Publishing
PO Box 470663
Tulsa, OK 74147-0663
www.kanemiller.com
www.edcpub.com
www.usbornebooksandmore.com

Library of Congress Control Number: 2019940423

Printed and bound in the United States of America

1 2 3 4 5 6 7 8 9 10

ISBN: 978-1-68464-037-9

Shine

Lily's Secret Audition

Holly Webb
Illustrated by Monique Dong

Kane Miller
A DIVISION OF EDC PUBLISHING

CHAPTER ONE
Like Mother, Like Daughter?

Lily Ferrars raced into school, looking forward to meeting up with her friends. She hadn't seen them for a whole sixteen hours, after all – chatting to Chloe on WhatsApp last night definitely didn't count. She galloped up the stairs to the Year Seven form room, grinning to herself. It seemed so weird that she'd fought against going to this school for ages and now she was desperate to get here!

Lily had planned to hate being at Shine

and to spend this year of exile not talking to anyone, but it hadn't quite worked out that way. She hadn't bargained on making three fantastic new friends in the first few weeks, and the atmosphere of the school was difficult to resist.

"Lily!" Sara bounded up behind her, with her face glowing, and Lily felt a teensy stab of jealousy. Sara had found out the day before that she'd gotten a part in a special Christmas run of *Mary Poppins* at a West End theatre. There was no doubt that Sara deserved to be at a stage school. Just looking at her now, star quality simply oozed out of her. Sara gave Lily a hug and the jealousy disappeared – Lily simply couldn't be anything but happy for such a good friend.

"Don't need to ask how you're feeling today!" she giggled. "Did you sleep at all last night?"

"Not much." Sara grinned. "It's so exciting. I can't wait for the letter to come from the theatre. Then it'll all be official. Contracts and everything."

They strolled into their classroom and loads of people called out their congratulations to Sara, who blushed but grinned even wider. Chloe and Bethany were sitting on the windowsill the four of them had claimed as their own.

"Yay, Sara!" Chloe called. "Sing 'A Spoonful of Sugar.' I want to hear how the professionals do it!"

Sara dumped her bag and scrambled up

next to them, making a face. "That's the one bad thing about this part – I've sung that song so many times. It used to be one of my favorites, but now I have to make it look as though I've never heard it before. On stage! Every day for weeks!"

"My mum said—" Lily started and then stopped, feeling embarrassed. Who wanted to hear what her mum said? But it seemed like the others did – they were all looking at her eagerly. Lily's mum was an actress, not a really famous one, but the kind that everyone recognizes from somewhere. Marina Ferrars was always on TV and she was hardly ever not working. Lily's dad was a lawyer who worked mostly with people in show business, so the Ferrars' house was always full of actor types – what Lily's grandad always called "luvvies." Lily hated it. Or she always had done, anyway. Her mum was certain that Lily was going to be an actress as well and so she'd started her in dance classes at two and a half, drama at three and singing at four. At first Lily had loved it, especially the acting, but for the last few years it hadn't been that much fun.

"You're so lucky having a mum who knows about all this stuff. What were you going to say?" Sara asked hopefully.

"Well, just that she was doing this play years ago, before I was born, and it was a really long run, so she knew the play backward. One night she was tired – I think she'd been to a party or something the night before – and she suddenly realized she was on stage in the middle of the second act, and she had absolutely no idea how she'd gotten there. She couldn't remember saying any of the lines, what she'd done in the interval, anything."

"What happened? Was she OK?" Chloe asked. The others were all leaning in, half-excited, half-terrified.

"She was so scared she froze up, but she was in the middle of a scene with the guy who was playing her husband and he sort of twisted some of the lines around so she could get back in without it being really obvious. She bought him a massive bar of chocolate the next day, she was so grateful."

"Wow." Sara shuddered. "I hope that doesn't happen to me."

"It won't," Lily said comfortingly. "She'd been doing that part for months. *Mary Poppins* isn't that long a run, is it? And you're alternating casts for the children. That's really good – you won't have a chance to get stale."

Bethany shook her head. "You know more about this stuff than anybody, Lily. You should set up an advice line for our year."

Lily flushed, wishing she'd never mentioned it. "Don't be silly," she said lightly. "I've never even had an audition." It wasn't exactly true, but then that was one of Lily's deepest, darkest secrets. "What about Chloe? You've had loads of work."

Chloe shook her head. "A whole lot of modeling and ads and one tiny part in a TV series. I don't know anything about theatre stuff."

Lily shrugged. "Well, I only know gossip from my mum and I'm sure she makes half of it up. In a few weeks' time Sara will be our theatre expert anyway!"

Lily felt a bit of a fraud when the others treated her like some sort of guru because of her mum. She hadn't even wanted to come to stage school! In Lily's last year at her primary school, her mum had brought home the prospectus for The Shine School for the Performing Arts. Everyone at her dance class was really jealous, but Lily was furious. She wanted to go on to the same school as all her friends, not spend the next five years training for a job she was never going to do.

There was a massive family row about it. Lily was totally expecting her dad to be on her side – he'd always backed her up when her mum tried to persuade her to go for parts before. So it was a huge shock when he said she should take the school's entrance audition.

"I won't do it!" Lily had snapped, feeling betrayed.

"I went to this school, Lily. You'll love it,

honestly," her mother pleaded.

"You don't understand!" Lily howled. "I don't want what you want! I don't want to be an actress – ever! And I'd hate stage school!"

"Lily, don't be like that," her father said in a tired voice. "You love your drama classes and I've seen you in your dance shows having a fantastic time. Why's this so different?"

"Because it's not doing it for fun," Lily tried to explain. "It means I'm trying to be a professional, and *I don't want to.*"

Her mum was crying by now and Lily didn't feel far off herself. She glared at her parents, hoping they'd back down, expecting that they would, like they normally did. It wasn't that she was exactly spoiled, but her mum and dad were both so busy all the time that she did tend to get what she wanted.

"You're not being fair." Her dad got up and pulled her onto his knee.

"Da-ad! I'm not five, you know!" Lily
protested, pretending to struggle.

"That's exactly my point, sweetheart. You're
old enough now for me to say this, Lily. You've
got a lot of talent and you'd be wasting it at a
normal school. Shine is a great place. Do the
audition and see what they say. It's one of the
hardest schools in the country to get into. If
they think you should be there, then I do too."

Lily slipped off his knee, hardly
knowing what to say. Her dad didn't give
out compliments lightly – he was always

complaining about actors who needed to be told how wonderful they were every five minutes. He'd never said anything like that before.

"Try it for a year, Lils," her mother suggested hopefully. "See if you get in, then just give it a go. Please?"

And so Lily had agreed – reluctantly. She was certain she'd never get through the audition anyway, so why worry? She'd be able to go to school with her friends after all.

She was surprised when she actually enjoyed the Shine audition, especially the speech and drama part. She almost felt sorry that she wouldn't be going there, though only for a moment. Her dad made an effort and phoned her from his office when she got home afterward. He seemed really excited. And her mum was over the moon when Lily grudgingly admitted the audition had been fun.

"But there were hundreds of people there – there's no way I'll get in, Mum, not when all the others have been sweating blood practicing. Everyone at ballet says you need to have a killer instinct to get in somewhere like Shine."

Her mum beamed. "I know what you mean, sweetie, but you're forgetting – the audition panel knew who you were. I added a letter with your application, explaining. There's no way they won't give you a place when they know you're my daughter. I'm one of their most famous graduates."

Lily stared at her in shock. It sounded like the whole thing had been a fix!

"You mean it has nothing to do with me at all?" she asked slowly. A strange feeling was creeping over her – almost as though she'd been cheated of something.

"Oh, not quite, darling." Her mum

laughed – a very
professional,
actressy laugh
that somehow set
Lily's teeth on
edge. "You'd have
had to be good,
but I'm sure your
connections gave you
an edge. You'll learn,
I'm afraid. In this business,
it's all about who you know."

"But what Dad said … about how if they
gave me a place it would mean I was supposed
to be there. He-he said I was talented. That
was why I agreed!"

"Oh, Lily, don't be such a silly little girl!"
Her mother sounded impatient. "You know
you're meant to be at a stage school – you
said yourself you enjoyed the audition! You're

following in my footsteps, that's all."

"I still might not get a place," Lily muttered defiantly. She was seething and her mother just didn't seem to get it. "And even if I do, you and Dad said I only had to go for a year. Then I'll leave!" She marched out of the room, her fingers clenched furiously, not noticing that back in the kitchen her mother was standing in the exact same pose, her nails digging into her palms.

★★★

Lily's relationship with her mother had always been up and down. Most of the time Lily adored her – she was such fun to be with – but she could be really pushy and difficult as well. Her dad said sometimes that they were just too similar to get along but Lily didn't see it. OK, so she looked like her mum, but that was it.

When she'd started at Shine at the beginning of term, they'd hit an all-time low. Marina Ferrars had insisted on taking Lily to school in full actress mode, expecting star treatment. She hadn't gotten it and the whole thing had been a disaster.

But the real nightmare started after Lily had finally managed to get rid of her mum. It was something she'd never told either of her parents about. A group of Year Eight girls who'd heard Marina Ferrars's little performance had ganged up on Lily, telling her she didn't deserve to be at Shine – that in fact she'd only gotten her place because her mum was famous.

The worst of it was that Lily knew they were right. Her mum had said so, after all. If she'd been completely rubbish at the audition, she wouldn't have gotten a place – her mum wasn't that important – but if it was down to a decision between her and someone else, Lily's mum's letter would have clinched it for her.

Only meeting Bethany and Sara had saved Lily from turning around and going straight home. She might have promised her dad a year, but not if the whole school was going to treat her like an impostor. He'd understand, especially if she told him what her mum had said about the letter after the audition. She'd been too angry, and somehow too ashamed, to talk to him about it at the time.

Bethany and Sara had done their best to convince her that the letter wouldn't have made any difference, and that Lizabeth, the Year Eight girl who'd really been picking on her, was just jealous. Well, Lily knew by now that they were totally right about Lizabeth, but she still wasn't sure she deserved to be at Shine and somehow that had stopped her from giving school everything she'd got.

CHAPTER TWO
The Most Unfair Thing Ever

Lily was starting to wonder if she was making a mistake. The rest of the Year Sevens were desperate to pull out all the stops in every class because who knew when the staff were on the lookout for someone to send to an audition? But Lily just couldn't quite bring herself to do it. Oh, occasionally a class would go brilliantly and she'd come out buzzing, but most of the time she was holding something back.

What was the point, after all? She was only

there because of her mum. Lily wasn't sure whether any of the staff had noticed that she wasn't really trying. It was funny though – being with Sara, Bethany and Chloe all the time, and seeing how much they loved Shine, was changing Lily almost without her realizing it. She was beginning to feel as if she might be passing up the best chance she'd ever been given – just to get back at her mum. The atmosphere at Shine was seeping under her skin and with the buzz about Sara's amazing part, how could Lily not feel excited? It seemed as though the whole school had heard the news, and all through the day whispers followed Sara and her friends wherever they went. Everyone thought that Sara's part in *Mary Poppins* was as good as settled – it was just a matter of her parents signing the contract.

Unfortunately, Sara's parents didn't see it that way and the next morning Sara wasn't waltzing into school. When Lily arrived, she found her curled up on the windowsill on her own, looking as though she'd been there forever.

"Wow! You're early. Dad dropped me off on his way to a meeting and I wasn't expecting anyone else to be here."

Sara didn't look up. She just muttered at her knees. "Yeah, well, I had to get out of the house. Couldn't stand it."

"What's the matter?" Lily asked anxiously, sitting next to Sara. Now that she was closer, she could see that Sara looked dreadful, really pale and red eyed. "What's happened?"

Sara uncurled slightly but still didn't look at Lily.

"I can't do the part. My parents won't let me."

"Wha-at?" Lily was amazed. Her mum was desperate for her to act. After five years of her subtly and then not-so-subtly trying to get Lily to audition for *anything*, parents who wouldn't let their daughter take a brilliant part seemed impossible. Lily's mum would have been turning cartwheels.

"Apparently," Sara spat bitterly, "it might have an unfortunate effect on my schoolwork. I've got a letter to give Ms. Purcell. Look." She drew an envelope out of her blazer pocket and stared at it with loathing.

"You can't actually be serious." Lily's eyes

were huge and black with horror. "They can't mean it."

"Yes, they can," Sara said grimly. "Well, it's not so much my dad, it's my mum. She's a teacher and she's obsessed with me doing well at school."

Lily nodded slowly. "I remember you saying you had to get a really good school report or they were going to move you at the end of term. But I never thought they'd do anything like this!"

"Neither did I. I suppose I should have expected it though. My mum wasn't exactly over the moon when she heard about the callback."

Bethany and Chloe walked in just then, and broke off chatting when they saw Sara and Lily's faces.

"What's up?" Chloe asked worriedly.

Lily glanced quickly at Sara. It was her news, but she didn't look as though she could face telling it again, so Lily gave the other two a quick rundown. They found it as hard to believe as she did.

Chloe got right to the point. "You mean you've actually got to go and tell Ms. Purcell you don't want the most fantastic part ever?"

"Yes." Sara sounded snappish, but the others didn't mind – she had plenty of reason. "Thanks, Chloe. Got it in one."

"You could just give the letter to her secretary," Bethany suggested. "Then you wouldn't have to actually – you know – *say it*."

Sara shook her head. "No, that would be worse. I'd just be waiting all day for a message to go and see her. She'll probably be in by now, won't she? I'll go and get it over with."

"Want us to come with you?" Bethany asked.

Sara shook her head. "No, it's OK. I'm not exactly good company. See you in a bit." She slid down from the windowsill and mooched out of the room, shoulders slumped.

The others watched her go, feeling shell-shocked.

"I just can't believe her parents would do that," Lily murmured, still staring at the door.

"It ought to be illegal," Chloe said furiously. "What if they give the part to Lizabeth instead?" Lizabeth had been up for the part as well and had sneakily tried to sabotage Sara's audition.

Chloe and Bethany kept discussing Sara's parents and how unbelievably awful they were, but Lily had zoned out. She couldn't help comparing Sara's mum with her own. They were both trying to control their daughters' lives but in different ways. It was as if she and Sara were opposites – Sara had desperately wanted to be at Shine and was fighting to stay, and Lily had never even wanted to be here.

Somehow, thinking that and remembering Sara's miserable face made her feel really guilty. The thoughts that had been niggling at the back of her mind for the last couple of weeks suddenly jumped into focus. She had no right to be at this school and not do her absolute best. Lily was beginning to realize how hard it would be to give up Shine after a year, with all her friends and the fantastic teaching. How could she go back to an everyday school and just do ballet and drama once a week? Even after only a few weeks at stage school, the idea was horrible.

However much Lily hated to admit it, her mum had been right – of course she still hadn't forgiven her for interfering, but Lily was starting to feel like Shine was where she was meant to be. It was embarrassing to admit it. *And I'm never telling Mum*, Lily thought furiously, not knowing whether she was angrier with her mum or herself.

Sara came back in, looking slightly less depressed, and the other three jumped down and went over to her.

"What did she say?" Lily asked anxiously. It would be too much if Ms. Purcell had a go at Sara when she was already so upset.

"Was she mad?" Chloe had had a run-in with Ms. Purcell earlier in the term and still thought she was totally scary.

"No, she was nice." Sara sounded surprised.

"She was really sympathetic. She said this kind of thing happened more often than I might think and she's going to call my mum at her school's break time and talk to her." She shrugged. "Not sure it'll do any good though. She's never met my mum."

Bethany put an arm around Sara's shoulders. "Well, I've never met your mum either, but I wouldn't like to get on the wrong side of Ms. Purcell. If anyone can make her see sense, Ms. Purcell can."

Sara grinned. "I know. I wish I could be there to hear them. Anyway, do you mind if we talk about something else? Somebody tell me something fun!"

Chloe squeaked. "Oh! I totally forgot. I saw Nathan as I was coming in this morning – he was in early for a piano lesson. He said to say hi. He definitely likes you, Sara!"

Sara couldn't help blushing happily. Then

she sighed. "He won't when he hears about *Mary Poppins* though. It sounds so babyish. 'My mummy says I'm not allowed.'"

Chloe looked apologetic. "Sorry, we were supposed to be getting off the subject. But I don't think that's true, Sara. He seems really nice. And it would be very cool to be going out with a Year Eight boy." She dropped her voice and hissed conspiratorially, "Better than any of this lot!"

Chloe's face was so funny that Sara and the others couldn't stop laughing – probably because they were so keyed up by what was happening. They kept breaking out into little sniggers every time one of the boys answered the register and it certainly added an extra spice to double science. Luckily Mrs. Taylor wasn't the strictest of teachers.

But by break time, Sara had gone quiet again. It was obvious that she was thinking about the principal calling her mum.

"You know what you need?" Lily said sternly, herding everyone to the cafeteria. "Sugar. Come on, I've got some sweets."

Bethany had a chocolate bar as well, so they sliced it up and shared it. Sara was just starting to look a bit less stressed when Lizabeth walked in, a gleeful expression on her face.

"Oh, no," Lily murmured. She had managed to stand up to Lizabeth the previous week when she was trying to have a go at Sara, but the tall blond girl still really scared her. She seemed to be an expert at picking up on people's weak points – a skill she was just about to demonstrate.

"So you're turning down the part then?" Lizabeth got straight to the point. How on earth did she know already?

"No," snapped Sara, suddenly thinking that if necessary she'd get herself adopted so that she could still take the part.

"That's not what I heard," Lizabeth said with a sneer. "Ms. Purcell must be really annoyed – this is just about as unprofessional as you can get!"

"More unprofessional than tricking someone into going to the wrong room for their audition because you know they're better than you?" another voice put in.

Lizabeth swung around angrily and found Nathan behind her.

"Get lost, Lizabeth. If Sara can't do the

part and they're silly enough to give it to you instead, I'm definitely telling everyone what you did. There's no way I'm spending six weeks on the same stage as someone like you. So take that smarmy little smile off your face."

Lizabeth gulped furiously and Nathan glared at her, backed up by all the others.

"No one would believe you," she spat at last, but she stormed off anyway.

"Have some!" Lily waved the candy bag at Nathan. "You've just earned it."

"Thanks!" He sat down. "Hey, I love the sour ones."

"How does everyone know about me not being able to do the part?" Sara asked anxiously.

Nathan shook his head. "Lizabeth's got Ms. Purcell's office bugged. No, actually Nadia had to go to the staff room about some homework she'd forgotten and she heard Mr. Lessing say something about it. It's true then? I was coming to find you anyway to ask."

Sara shrugged miserably. "I – don't know. My parents don't want me to do it, but Ms. Purcell reckoned she might be able to convince my mum."

"It would be a real shame if you can't. You're really good – better than all the others were." He fidgeted uncomfortably, as though he'd like to say something else. Chloe was just starting to make "Let's get out of here!" faces at Lily and Bethany when Miss Clare, Ms. Purcell's secretary, appeared at the cafeteria door, clearly looking for someone. Sara was staring at the table like it was the most interesting thing she'd ever seen and didn't notice, but Bethany bounced up and ran to check who she was searching for. She was back in seconds. "Sara, you have to go to the office now! Come on!"

Everyone grabbed their stuff and raced out of the cafeteria, carrying Sara along with them. They surged down the stairs and arrived at the principal's office panting and looking hopeful. Miss Clare was back behind her desk, and she grinned.

"You'd better go in, Sara. The rest of you will have to stay out here. And that door's soundproof, Chloe," she added, as Chloe attempted to accidentally on purpose lean next to it.

It seemed like hours before Sara fumbled her way out of the office, looking blissed out.

"They said yes!"

Lily squawked delightedly, hugging her. "They must have done, for you to look like that!"

Sara nodded happily and beamed at Nathan, who was looking relieved.

"Bad news though – we have to have extra remedial classes to catch up on anything we miss. The school's going to arrange a tutor for both of us at the theatre, so we can work when we're not needed in rehearsals." Strangely enough, Nathan didn't look too worried by this...

Lily watched her friend thoughtfully. She knew how stressful the audition had been for Sara – even before all these problems with her parents. But just look at her now – Sara's dreams had come true! Lily was beginning to feel like she might be really missing out.

CHAPTER THREE
A Change of Heart

Everyone was so pleased that Sara would be able to do the part after all – the relief was incredible. It made them giggly for the rest of lunch. Lily stopped worrying about her life choices and just went with the madness. It was nice to zone out and watch Chloe trying to build a lettuce tower from the remains of her salad.

But they all sobered up slightly when they got into the studio for drama class.

Mr. Lessing was already there and Ms. Shaw was with him, watching interestedly as they poured in. She'd been introduced to all the Year Sevens soon after they arrived at Shine, and everyone wanted to impress her.

Ms. Shaw ran The Shine Agency, which represented all the pupils at the school. She was the one currently negotiating Sara's contract with the Theatre Royal. Was she here because she needed to talk to Sara? But she could have just asked for her to come down to the agency, which was in the building next door, where all the part-time courses were held. Lily knew it was much more likely that she was here scoping out possibles for an audition!

"Why didn't I brush my hair at lunch?" Chloe moaned, frantically trying to tidy up her curls with her fingers while hiding behind Bethany.

"Don't lurk behind Bethany, you muppet," Sara sniggered. "You're about a foot taller than she is! You look like you've been chopped off at the knees."

"If being a star in musicals makes you this rude all the time, Sara Sinclair, I'll sabotage your next audition myself. She isn't *that* much taller than me." Bethany was slightly sensitive about being tiny.

"You're standing on tiptoe now," Sara said, giggling.

"I'm not!" Bethany scowled and stood normally again.

"Hey, stop bickering! I want to know why Ms. Shaw's here. Has anyone heard any gossip about a part?" Lily couldn't help feeling excited. The timing was kind of weird – the school's agent was there looking interested, just as Lily had almost decided she was going to turn over a new leaf. Maybe this part was meant for her!

"Nope." Sara shook her head.

Bethany laughed. "Sara, you haven't heard anything anyone's said at all for the last three days!" But she didn't say it meanly, and Sara grinned and shrugged.

"Yeah, that's true. Sorry, have I been a pain?"

"Don't be silly. We'd all be the same," Lily said lightly, wondering if it might be her turn next. She just had this feeling... "So no one's heard anything?"

"Not a thing." Chloe shook her head vigorously, which completely undid all her frantic finger combing. "Oh well. They'll just have to want the Little Orphan Annie look."

"Is everyone here yet?" Mr. Lessing looked up from his papers. "OK, everyone, I'm sure you'll have noticed that Ms. Shaw is here. And yes, she is on the lookout for audition candidates." A small flurry of excitement ran through the class as various people said they'd told other people so. "But this doesn't mean we'll be doing anything different. Ms. Shaw will just be observing. Then toward the end of the class, she and I will have a quick discussion about who we think she should be shortlisting to audition for this particular part. Any questions?"

Carmen, one of the twins, shyly put up her hand.

"Yes, Carmen?"

"Are we allowed to know what the part is?" she asked excitedly. Mr. Lessing looked at Ms.

Shaw, who nodded, and smiled at Carmen.

"There are two. It's a new TV drama, *Little Women*. We've been asked to send girls to audition for the parts of Beth and Amy. There are quite a few smaller parts too – for boys and girls. Most of you probably know the story?"

Some of the girls nodded, but most of the boys looked blank.

"I suppose it is a bit of an old book. There've been a couple of films too, but this is a really exciting new series. Big budget too. Wonderful locations and costumes, a real experience for anyone involved." Ms. Shaw sounded delighted about it all.

Chloe exchanged an eager look with Ella, Carmen's twin. Lily remembered talking to Ella on their very first day about how much they both loved costume drama – anything that involved serious dressing up!

Lily stared at Ms. Shaw, biting her lip between her teeth. *Little Women* had been one of her favorite books since they'd read bits of it last year at school. She'd bought her own copy to read the rest and it had made her cry, even if it had been written nearly a hundred and fifty years ago. She loved the story of the four sisters, who'd lived during the American Civil War. Almost everything the March girls did was old-fashioned and odd and nothing like Lily's life, but she loved their big, funny family and how different they all were. She just *had* to be shortlisted for this audition – even if her mum would never let her hear the end of it!

"So everybody needs to be showing their full potential in this class!" Was it Lily's imagination or was Mr. Lessing looking at her when he said that? Maybe he'd noticed that she hadn't really been trying! Lily focused on doing her absolute best.

They'd started working on character development over the last couple of classes. They had a book of short scenes and Mr. Lessing divided them up into groups to work on one together, often getting them to swap the parts around in the middle or do other things that made them think about the words they were actually saying. He'd said last time that you couldn't really understand a scene properly unless you'd played all the different parts in it. Lily wasn't totally sure he was right – there must be some parts that depended on not understanding the other person's point of view? How could you act an argument if you agreed with the person you were meant to be fighting with? But when she had said that to Mr. Lessing, he just beamed at her infuriatingly and said that was where the acting came in.

Today, he put Lily in a group with Chloe, Ella and Sam, a friend of Chloe's whose hair was just about redder than hers. He was even more of a joker than Chloe too. Lily hoped they were both going to behave – today's class wasn't for messing around, however funny they usually were.

Luckily Sam seemed too grumpy for jokes. "More parts for girls!" he muttered. "When's the starring role in the next Bond film coming along? That's what I want to know!"

"You'd make a great evil sidekick," Chloe agreed. "There ought to be more ginger villains." She put her head to one side and gazed at Sam, who was glaring crossly at her. "Yeah, that's the perfect evil face, I can see it working."

"Chloe!" Lily hissed crossly. "Ms. Shaw's here, remember! We need to concentrate!"

Chloe looked surprised. "OK. OK! Since you're so keen. Which one of these are we doing?"

"Page thirty-four." Lily sighed and Ella gave her a sympathetic look. Chloe was lovely but ditzy. And it was hard to tell, but grumpy Sam might just be even worse than hyper Sam…

It was time for drastic action. "Sam, there's a great part in this for you," Lily said sweetly, modeling herself on her mum, who could charm people into doing almost anything. "Not quite James Bond but a gangster. Then Ella can be your sidekick, and Chloe and me will do the two girls. OK? We'll probably have to swap in a bit anyway."

They worked on the scene for a couple of minutes and Sam cheered up when he got to use his terrible over-the-top New York accent.

Mr. Lessing was working his way around the groups, getting everyone to try different things. Ms. Shaw was wandering about too, and Lily couldn't help keeping an anxious eye on her. What was she looking for? Was there anything Lily should be trying to do? Probably ignoring her... Lily returned to concentrating on the scene, trying to sound like the silly, giggly high-society girl who hadn't realized she was actually being kidnapped.

"That's good, Lily." She jumped as Mr. Lessing spoke just behind her – she hadn't noticed him. "Now try doing it as though actually you know perfectly well what's going on, but you're just pretending not to."

Lily nodded. "So they can escape? OK."

"Do *I* know?" Chloe asked eagerly. This was the best thing about acting classes – trying out all these different tricks.

"Umm, no. See if you can stay being dim,"

Mr. Lessing said thoughtfully.

"Shouldn't be hard," growled Sam, getting his revenge.

"Thank you, Sam. You and Ella try and up the menace, please. More like you're mafia villains."

Mr. Lessing listened appreciatively as they went through the scene again. He nodded. "Nice. Now, swap all the parts around. You try being the gangster this time, Lily." Then he disappeared to watch the next group.

"You better not think I'm playing one of those silly girls," Sam said just as Ms. Shaw walked past, and Lily could have murdered him, which would have been in character at least.

About ten minutes before the end of the lesson, Mr. Lessing and Ms. Shaw huddled themselves in a corner with a load of notes Ms. Shaw had been making. Everyone tried desperately to hear what they were saying, while looking as though they were still carrying on with the gangster scene. Lily's group practically went to pieces, with her and Ella and Chloe all whispering their lines in case they could catch anything from the other side of the studio. Lily was pretty certain Ms. Shaw had just pointed at their group. What was Mr. Lessing saying?

"All right, gather around all of you – the suspense is over!" Mr. Lessing was grinning. "Ms. Shaw would like to have a word."

The agent smiled at everyone. "I'm sorry that this is a very short shortlist – we're sending people to audition from other years as well, of course. For the moment, I think we'll be considering, let me see –" she checked her list – "Chloe, Emily and Lauren. Don't worry, the rest of you, I'm sure there'll be lots of other chances soon. I'll sort out audition times for those three and let you know."

Lily was frozen. She could see Bethany and Sara and the twins hugging Chloe, and congratulating Emily and Lauren, but she just couldn't make herself join in. She'd been so sure about being shortlisted! It had been *her* audition! It felt like it still should be. What had Chloe done that she hadn't? Mr. Lessing had said that she'd done really well in the scene, hadn't he?

She realized that Chloe was looking at her, clearly expecting her to say something, and she forced herself to smile. "Well done!" she whispered, totally failing to sound as though she was pleased. Then she gave herself a little shake. She wasn't being fair on Chloe – but it was just so hard! She met a sympathetic look from Bethany and felt even worse. Was her disappointment that obvious? She summoned up every ounce of acting ability she owned – which was quite a lot – and gave Chloe a much more realistic grin. "So which of the little women are you going to be? The snotty little one or the saintly one who nearly dies?" she asked, and Chloe looked relieved.

"Nearly time for the bell, everyone, you can go early today," Mr. Lessing called. "See you on Friday."

He waved them out and started packing up his things. Bethany, Sara and Chloe were heading for the door, chatting eagerly about Chloe's fantastic luck. Lily trailed after them.

Then suddenly she turned back. "Keep going! I just want to ask Mr. Lessing something – I'll catch you up at registration," she called.

Bethany looked back curiously, but Lily just waved and kept going. Lily dithered about near the door, pretending to look for something in her bag until everyone else had gone, and then she approached Mr. Lessing, who was chatting with Ms. Shaw. Lily had no idea what she was going to say – she was hoping that something would just come to her.

Ms. Shaw smiled at her. "Did you want Mr. Lessing, Lily?"

Lily looked surprised – she hadn't expected Ms. Shaw to know her name. Perhaps that was a good sign?

"Um, yes," she murmured nervously. "I was just wondering – um. I wanted to know…" she faltered. How on earth could she ask why she hadn't been shortlisted too? It would sound so conceited.

She stared at her feet, so as not to have to look at Mr. Lessing, who always seemed to be laughing at her, and said as calmly as she could, "I was wondering if there was any way I could change your mind about the shortlist." Being calm suddenly stopped working and Lily looked up pleadingly. "I-I just really want this audition!"

Mr. Lessing was looking thoughtful, which was good – at least he wasn't furious with her.

He exchanged a glance with Ms. Shaw.

"This is – unexpected, Lily," he said slowly.

"I know. I'm sorry," Lily muttered, wondering if this was the kind of thing you could get thrown out of stage school for.

"I have to tell you, Ms. Shaw did notice you when she was watching the class. She was very impressed and thought you would be excellent auditioning for Beth March."

Lily glanced up delightedly and caught Ms. Shaw's eye. She was looking amused, but she wiped the smile off her face at once.

"We considered putting you on the shortlist, but I had to tell Ms. Shaw that I just didn't think you were committed enough for an important audition like this."

Lily felt the tears burning at the back of her eyes. She was too late! Why hadn't she decided to make an effort earlier? "Oh. I see," she said miserably, turning to go.

"Lily." It was Ms. Shaw, calling her back. "Mr. Lessing's right – it is unexpected, a student asking to be given an audition. But I have to say, it shows a certain amount of commitment. The commitment we're worried that you can't give us. Don't you think so?" she asked the drama teacher.

Mr. Lessing nodded. "You do agree, Lily, don't you, that you just haven't been trying in my classes so far? Oh, the occasional class, you stand out, but most of the time you can hardly be bothered."

"I'm sorry," Lily muttered, staring at the floor again.

"So why

should I put you forward for a wonderful opportunity like this? Seriously, Lily, tell me." Mr. Lessing's voice was stern.

Lily dragged her eyes up from the floor. "Because I've decided to try," she said in a very small voice. It was so embarrassing to have to say all of this. "I didn't want to be here at first, but now I really, really do. I'll try so hard. Even if I'm not right for this part, I will keep trying in classes, honestly. And I would be good," she added with a flash of pride.

Ms. Shaw had a pleased sort of look on her face, but Mr. Lessing still looked doubtful. Lily wasn't expecting the answer she got.

"OK. We'll put you in. But you've made a deal, Lily, and you have to stick to it. I'm going to be watching – just remember that."

She nodded frantically, hardly able to believe he'd said yes.

"Go on then. We'll let you know the

audition time." Lily stumbled toward the door, and Mr. Lessing called after her, "Don't forget – I'm expecting a lot from you now!"

Lily shut the studio door behind her, her stomach churning. That counted as possibly the most stressful five minutes of her life. And now, of course, she had to explain it to the others.

CHAPTER FOUR
Breaking the News

Lily walked through the corridors to the Year Seven form room, half hugging herself with delight at the thought of the audition. It was so strange after all these years of refusing to try, but this part just seemed to be calling to her. The other half of her was worrying, though. What on earth was she going to say to Chloe? Whatever she said was going to sound really weird, but she had to say something. She went into their form room a little nervously.

Everyone was packing stuff away in their lockers while they waited for Miss James, but Bethany saw Lily come in.

"Hey! What did you need to talk to Mr. Lessing about? Is everything OK?" Her sweet, concerned expression immediately made Lily feel better. She glanced around and saw that Sara and Chloe were looking worried too. Lily took a deep breath.

"I'm fine," she said slowly. "But I've got to tell you something and I think you might be a bit ticked off with me – especially you, Chloe."

Chloe shook her head, looking confused. "Why? What is it?"

"I stayed behind because I wanted to ask Mr. Lessing and Ms. Shaw to change their minds and let me audition too," Lily gabbled – it wasn't surprising that it took the others a little while to work out what she was saying.

"You did what?" Chloe said, sounding a bit

dazed by the idea.

"You're not cross?" Lily asked anxiously.

"No, I'm just – I don't know – amazed! I
can't believe you did that!" Chloe's blue eyes
were huger than ever as she stared at Lily as if
she was some strange performing animal. She
seemed to be expecting Lily to laugh and say
she was just making it up.

"I know. I can't believe it either." Lily shook
her head at her own daring. "You'll laugh, but
I had this really funny feeling about this part. I
couldn't just leave it."

Sara leaned forward. "But Lily, what did they say? I mean, I don't really know Ms. Shaw, and Mr. Lessing, he's nice and everything, but I can't see him just turning around and changing his mind. He's not like that."

Lily shuddered, remembering. "He didn't. He went all strict and asked what made me think they should do something like that for me. It was scary." She didn't want to tell the others what Mr. Lessing had said about her not trying. Not yet anyway – it would mean she would have to explain about her mum and not really wanting to be at Shine. Lily just wasn't ready to talk about something so important and difficult, although she thought maybe she would tell them all eventually.

"So – what happened?" Chloe asked. "What did you say?"

Lily shrugged, wishing she could think of something more convincing. "I just begged," she said slowly. "Ms. Shaw said she'd noticed me in the class anyway, so I guess they just changed their minds."

Bethany was looking at her skeptically but didn't say anything. Lily flashed her a grateful glance. *I will tell you, I promise*, she thought, feeling mean. *Just not now.*

"Well, however you did it, I think it's brilliant," Chloe said cheerfully. "The audition will be much more fun with you there than it would with just Emily and Lauren."

Lily grinned at her, feeling so relieved. She'd thought that Chloe's feelings might be hurt, but she hadn't counted on her friend's sunny nature.

"Hey!" Chloe squeaked excitedly. "We might even end up both being cast! You as Beth and me as Amy. That would be fab!"

Lily had been focusing so much on getting the audition and then telling the others, that she hadn't really thought about what her parents' reaction would be. It hit her as she was waiting for her train. What was her mum going to say? Oh well, at least she had some time to think about it – her mum was away filming and wouldn't be back until the next day. It would just be her and Dad. Lily couldn't wait for him to get home. OK, so it would be embarrassing to admit that they'd been right all along and she did want an acting career – but he was going to be so proud of her!

Lily's dad had deliberately gotten home earlier than usual from the office because of her mum being away. Usually he was at work till all hours.

He greeted her conspiratorially as she walked in the door, waving a sheaf of papers. "All the local takeout menus, Lily! Your mum's not here to lecture us about a healthy diet and the whole 'carbs are poison' thing, so what do you fancy? Pizza? Chinese?"

Lily's stomach rumbled on cue. "Don't mind as long as we can have ice cream as well," she bargained. "We have to, Dad – I'm celebrating!"

"Celebrating what?" Her dad grinned wryly. "Surviving another day at the nightmare school?"

Lily shuffled her feet. Had she been that bad about going to Shine? It seemed hard to believe now.

"Er, no…" How could she put this? "I've, um, got an audition." She fluttered her eyelashes at her dad. Was he going to rub it in?

"Seriously?" he asked, looking shocked. "You're not pulling my leg?"

"Uh-uh."

"Lily! That's brilliant! What's it for? I thought you swore to me you were never going to move a muscle in acting classes unless you were forced to! How've you ended up with an audition?"

"I was trying not to try – if you see what I mean," Lily admitted. "But – oh, the classes are really good sometimes. They give us fun stuff to do. And all my friends are really into it. I told you about Sara, didn't I?"

"The one who's going to be in *Mary Poppins*? Yes, yes, you did." Her dad was nodding eagerly. It struck Lily that her dad probably knew more about Sara's great part than Sara's dad did, which seemed awful.

"Well, her parents said no! She was really gutted – you can't imagine. But Ms. Purcell sorted it out for her. Anyway, it just made me think about everything." Lily looked up at her dad and quickly down again, twisting her fingers. "I decided you were right. You and Mum." It was even more of a wrench to admit that.

Suddenly she squeaked as her dad swept her up in a huge hug. "You can have as much ice cream as you want, Lily, my love! I'm so proud of you. You needed to find it out for yourself, but wow, I'm glad you did. You'd have been wasted doing anything else. You know that, don't you?"

"Maybe," Lily agreed cautiously, not wanting to commit herself to too much.

Her dad suddenly sobered up. "But listen, if this audition doesn't go well, promise me you won't take it to heart like the other time, OK?

You know how many setbacks your mum's had?"

Lily nodded.

"There's too many to count." Her dad chuckled. "But it's just something you have to deal with."

"I've got a good feeling about this one," Lily said. "But, yeah. I will try not to pin my hopes on it. It'll be hard though," she added, frowning. "It just seems so right."

"Hey, you haven't even told me what it's for yet!" Lily's dad did the comedy face-slap thing that he'd always used to make her giggle as a little girl.

"It's a TV series of *Little Women*. You remember, that book I loved reading at school? It's a really big budget thing apparently. Ms. Shaw – she's our agent – she was ever so excited about it."

Lily's dad nodded excitedly. "Yes, I've heard

about it. It's going to be a real 'classic serial' sort of thing – the kind they want the whole family to watch together. They'll probably show it on Sunday evenings. The writer's one of our clients."

"The writer?" Lily looked confused. "It's already written!"

Her dad grinned. "Yes, but they'll adapt it loads – you know that, Lily. Mostly when something's written as a book there isn't enough dialogue for film or TV."

"I suppose. I hope they don't spoil it though," Lily said anxiously. She didn't want her favorite book changed too much!

"Don't worry. Bill, our client, he's very good. Very subtle. You won't be able to spot where the original ends and he starts! So are you up for one of the sisters?"

"Mmm, Amy or Beth. But Ms. Shaw thought I'd be really good for Beth. I look right, anyway – if I was playing Amy I'd have to go blond! My friend Chloe's going for the audition too, and she'd be really good as Amy, I think. She's got red hair though, so she'd have to wear a wig. At least, I think so. I'm pretty sure the book says she's blond. I've always thought of her as having blond hair and Beth as dark like me."

"Your mum's going to be over the moon," Lily's dad commented as he riffled through the takeout menus again. "Now, which of these do you reckon?"

★ ★ ★

"Over the moon" turned out to be an understatement. Lily's mum was ecstatic. She got home really late on Thursday night, after Lily was in bed. Lily's dad wanted to give her the chance to break the news so he didn't say anything, which meant that when Lily trailed sleepily down to breakfast on Friday morning, her mum was opening the mail with no idea of the shock she was about to get.

Lily gave her mum a kiss, grabbed the cereal box and sat down. She had just about worked out that the familiar-looking logo on the envelope her mum was opening meant it was from school, and was dozily wondering why school was sending letters home (she really wasn't a morning person), when her mother yelped and sat bolt upright. *That* woke her up.

"What's the matter?" she gasped, grabbing at the bottle of milk she'd just seriously over-poured onto the cereal.

"You! You've got an audition! Lily!" Her mother was still scanning the letter, trying to take it all in.

"Oh, that. Yes." Lily nodded. Thank goodness – she'd thought for a second she might have been expelled.

"'Oh, that'! Lily! How can you just say 'Oh, that'!? This is amazing news! Why didn't you tell me?" Her mother was clutching the letter as if it was a winning lottery ticket.

"You weren't here!" Lily protested, looking to her dad for backup.

"Darling, you should have phoned my mobile. Dave, why didn't you phone me?" She glared at Lily's dad jokingly. "Honestly! Tell me everything!" She leaned forward eagerly.

Somehow it was much harder to talk to her mum about it all. Lily had rattled on to her dad for ages over their pizza the night before, but all the arguments she and her mum had had about her not doing auditions over the years made it hard to open up now.

She shrugged awkwardly. "There's not much to tell yet. There are four of us from our year going for it and some older girls too. Mr. Lessing saw us all yesterday and he said that the production company are sending over scripts for the audition, hopefully today. Which is good because then we have the weekend to look over them. And the audition will be one day next week, after school probably."

"But Lily, what happened to make you change your mind?" Her mum's voice was almost pleading. "All those other auditions — why did you say no to those but not this one?"

How could she say it? *Because you were*

trying to force me! Lily gazed mulishly at her cereal and her mother sighed.

"Well, if you were going to pick one thing to audition for, Lily, you've certainly picked well. This series is going to be amazing – it's already got a fantastic cast lined up and there's a lot of buzz about it. It'll be a wonderful opportunity for you, working with some of these people." She beamed delightedly. It was as though she'd managed to put Lily's strange attitude completely out of her mind.

"Slow down, Mum, I haven't even done the audition yet!" Lily said grumpily. Her mother seemed to be taking over, as usual.

"Exactly," her father put in. "Don't jump the gun, Marina. There'll be hundreds of girls going for these parts. I know you'll audition brilliantly, Lily, but you can never tell who they'll choose."

"Oh, nonsense!" Lily's mother waved this away impatiently. "Of course Lily will get it. She's got the talent *and* the background. This is a very prestigious series, darling. It's going to be fantastic to start your career with this – it'll get you really well known."

"But, Mum—" Lily was starting to get panicky already. Her excitement about the audition was ebbing away and being replaced by a numb feeling.

"Now, who do I know who's involved with this one?" her mother murmured, ignoring Lily's worried face. She gathered up her mail decisively. "Don't worry, Lily. I'll make sure you're perfectly prepared for the audition. We can work on the script together this weekend. Isn't it lucky my filming's finished?" She floated out of the room humming happily to herself, leaving Lily and her dad staring across the table at each other in dismay.

★★★

Lily couldn't help worrying all the way to school. It was really nice that her parents were proud and excited about the audition – she couldn't imagine having parents like Sara's, who didn't seem to be at all interested! – but her mum was *too* excited somehow. She seemed to be taking the audition as a personal challenge, when Lily didn't really want it to be anything to do with her!

Am I being mean? Lily wondered to herself, getting off the train and trailing up the platform. It would just be nice to do this audition as herself and not as her mother's daughter. That was the problem with her mum – she would keep on treating Lily almost like she was a part of her.

Lily brightened up as she walked through the school doors. What could her mum do? It wasn't as if her mum really had anything to do with the audition – the school was arranging it. And some of her own excitement, which had been banished by her mum's enthusiasm, started to creep back.

The audition script would probably arrive today and Lily couldn't wait to see it. She just hoped her dad was right about the scriptwriter and the book wasn't changed a lot. She'd been rereading it in bed the last couple of nights and she loved it so much. She had lots of questions too, like would there be any filming in America and would they have to do American accents? It was an American story, after all. She giggled at the thought of Sam's gangster accent in the drama class. She couldn't imagine the sweet March sisters talking like that!

Luckily there was an acting class that afternoon, and Chloe and Lily were determined to get there early. They'd dragged Sara and Bethany out of the ballet studio at warp speed, and bullied them into changing back into school uniforms way faster than usual. Sara practically broke her neck running up the stairs with her shoes only half on.

"I told you he wouldn't be here yet!" she moaned to Lily, massaging her ankle. "You made us rush all this way for nothing." But she didn't really mind that much. She and Nathan had their first rehearsals for *Mary Poppins* that weekend, and she was aiming to be at least an hour early, so she understood how Lily and Chloe felt.

As soon as Mr. Lessing walked in the door, Lily and Chloe pounced on him, and Emily and Lauren, the other two girls up for the audition, weren't far behind.

"Have you got the script?" Chloe demanded, skidding across the polished floor.

Mr. Lessing grinned. He was always teasing. "Possibly, possibly. What's it worth?"

Lily and the others gazed at him with identical reproachful expressions. "Oh, all right. You could have been a bit nicer to me. You know, 'Good afternoon, Mr. Lessing. Isn't it a lovely day?' *then* mugging me for the script – that would have been better, but since you're looking at me like starved kittens… Yes. Four copies of the audition script are currently in my bag."

The four of them stared at the bag, more like wolves than kittens. They looked as though they were seriously considering knocking him to the ground and grabbing it.

"You're getting your copies at the end of the lesson and not a minute earlier." He ignored their groaning. "Can you all stay after school, do you think? I know it's short notice, but I'd like to do a bit of coaching. Then you can take the scripts away and work on them some more over the weekend."

They nodded eagerly. Of course they'd stay. Lily beamed at Chloe. Being coached for an audition for a part she was desperate for! Why on earth had she *ever* made a fuss about stage school?

CHAPTER FIVE
The Perfect Part

After registration, Lily and Chloe dashed back to the drama studio, their scripts gripped tightly in their hands. Even just holding the script was exciting! They hadn't had much time to look at them, but the dire warnings printed on the covers about them being the property of the production company and not to be shown to anyone made it all seem so real.

Emily and Lauren arrived a couple of minutes later, reverently clutching their scripts too. Lily didn't know either of them that well – they'd chatted occasionally, but that was all. She was so glad that she was doing this with Chloe. Every so often she couldn't help thinking about her previous audition experience – which had been a nightmare – but at least this time she had a friend with her. At the moment she was refusing to worry about the fact that, actually, she and Chloe were competing for these roles. It was just too much. If Chloe got a part and she didn't, then Lily would just have to try and be happy for her…

Mr. Lessing was coaching the Year Eight girls separately as he needed small groups, so it was just the four of them.

"Just take five minutes to read through the scene, girls. Try and get a feel for it. Have you read the book, any of you?"

Lily nodded and so did Emily, but Chloe and Lauren looked embarrassed.

"Don't worry, it doesn't matter. Just bear
in mind that Amy's the youngest sister, quite
spoiled and very self-conscious about not
having a lot of money compared to her school
friends. Beth's different – a year or so older,
very shy and quiet. It's a more difficult part,
really. She's so saintly and mouse-like that you'll
have to try hard to get anything interesting
out of her. You're all reading for both parts
at the audition, but I'd guess that each of you
feels closer to one of the girls. That doesn't

necessarily mean that the casting team will agree with you though!"

Lily couldn't help feeling that she was more the Beth type and Chloe was an Amy. Not that her friend was spoiled, but she certainly wasn't saintly and mouse-like! She wasn't sure about Emily and Lauren yet.

Lily had seen lots of her mum's scripts lying around, so the layout of the lines and the directions was pretty familiar. The scene was one she remembered well from the book, where Beth catches scarlet fever from trying to help the children of a poorer family in the town. Her older sisters, Meg and Jo, feel really guilty because they should have been helping instead of Beth. Amy is miserable because it means she has to go and stay with their scary old aunt, so as not to catch the fever herself.

It was so weird to see the scene as a script rather than a book. But Lily could see that her dad was right – the scriptwriter had really kept to the feel of the book. He'd just gotten rid of a lot of the wordier bits that Lily had to admit she'd skimmed through anyway! She looked up eagerly at Mr. Lessing when she finished reading.

He grinned at her. "Everyone finished? What do you think?"

"I love Amy!" Chloe was practically bouncing up and down. "I mean – if I got cast as Beth it would be fab, but Amy's really fun. She's got this catty side to her, I really like it! Lily, she doesn't go all sweet and nice in the end, does she?"

"A bit. They all do really," Lily admitted. "But there's a sequel and she ends up falling in love with the boy next door. Beth dies," she added impressively.

"Oh wow," Lauren put in. "Would whoever gets that part have to do a deathbed scene then? That would be weird."

"I'm not sure how far the series is taking the story," Mr. Lessing admitted. "I've a feeling that the sequel is set a few years later, so even if they do go that far, they might have another actress playing Beth, and I'm sure they will for Amy. Let's read through anyway. We'll split into pairs. Chloe, you read Amy as you like her so much, and Lily, you can do Beth – you'll have to fill in Jo and Meg too. I'll work with Emily and Lauren for a bit, and then I'll come to you."

Chloe and Lily practiced reading the scene through a couple of times, and Lily really felt that Chloe's natural sparkly character came through as Amy, who loved wearing beautiful clothes and having nice things.

"You're doing her so well," she exclaimed as they finished the scene for the second time, with Amy grumbling about how unfair everything was.

Chloe grinned. "I think Mr. Lessing's right – Beth's much harder. She's just so *nice*, isn't she?"

"You don't feel you're qualified for acting nice, Chloe?" Mr. Lessing said, laughing at her as he walked over to them.

Chloe shook her head. "Not really," she admitted, giggling.

"Well, let's see how Lily manages. Start again for me."

They read it through again, Lily trying very hard to sound more than just "nice" – she didn't want her character to be boring. Beth had to come back from looking after a sick baby and tell her sisters that she thought she had scarlet fever. *How would she really sound?* Lily wondered. Her lines were brave and she was worried about Amy catching the disease, but she must be scared really. Lily tried to read it as though Beth wasn't as brave inside as she acted outside, and at the end of the scene she looked hopefully at Mr. Lessing. Had it worked?

"Excellent, both of you." He was nodding and looking pleased. "Especially you, Lily, that was a very clever reading. You were really thinking about what was going on inside her. Keep doing it like that, you're bringing a lot out of it. Chloe, I'm sorry to say this, but you're right – you do just have a natural advantage playing Amy! Swap around now and see how you feel playing the other sister. You'll find it interesting."

It *was* interesting. Lily could see why Chloe enjoyed being Amy so much – it was quite fun being selfish and trying hard to pretend not to be! But she couldn't help thinking that Beth was the more challenging, rewarding role.

It was hard to believe that an hour had passed when Mr. Lessing finally looked at the clock and sent them home. "Try and start learning the words," he told them. "You'll be able to have the scripts at the audition, but you don't want to be staring down at the page all the time. And keep thinking about what you want to bring out of the lines. I'd like to do some coaching with each of you separately as well." He checked his diary. "I can do before school and lunchtime on Monday – Lily, can you get in by eight thirty?"

★★★

Lily and Chloe were buzzing with enthusiasm as they walked to the station. "I hope the audition's soon," Chloe said, "like really early next week. I just want to get on and do it."

Lily nodded. "Will you work on it lots at home?" she asked.

"Definitely! I'll get my mum to read the other parts. She'll be really excited." Chloe beamed, but Lily couldn't hold back a tiny shudder. *Her* mum would be excited too. And she had said she would be home all weekend to work on the script with her. Lily had a feeling that this weekend might just be hard work...

★★★

She was right. Her mum demanded the script as soon as she got home and Lily handed it over reluctantly. It made it feel like it was *hers*, not Lily's. She didn't really want her mum interfering, but it would be silly to turn down coaching from a professional actress, wouldn't it? That's what she had to think of her mum as – just extra coaching.

"This is wonderful, Lily!" Her mum's voice was so excited. "Come on, let's read through it together."

"What? Now?" Lily asked helplessly.

"Of course!"

"Can't it wait until tomorrow? I've got

homework and – and stuff," Lily muttered.

Her mum gazed at her in disappointment.
"Don't you *want* to do this?"

"Yes, but—" How could she explain?
"Tomorrow, OK? I've just had a coaching
session and I'm really tired." She snatched
the script out of her mum's hand and raced
off upstairs before her mum could complain.
Maybe tomorrow she'd feel up to it. Right
now she just wanted to curl up on her bed and
think herself back to America, a hundred and
fifty years before. On her *own*.

★★★

Lily's mum hardly let her finish breakfast the
next morning – she seemed to be channeling
some scary energy from somewhere and she
was clearly desperate to get going on the
script. Unfortunately Lily had even less energy
than she normally did in the morning, after a

night of weird dreams about auditions where she turned up with her skirt tucked into her underwear.

Shooed into the living room while still eating a piece of toast, Lily sighed and collapsed on the sofa.

"Right, I've copied the script," her mum said briskly. "You don't mind, do you, darling? I got it from your room while you were having a shower."

Lily gaped, too furious to speak. Of course she minded! But there seemed no point in having a fight about it. She shook her head dumbly.

"It's much easier if we both have a copy. Then I can write notes on this one."

Notes? Her mum was taking this so seriously. Not for the first time, Lily began to wish the school had sent the letter about the audition to her dad.

"Now, you're auditioning for both parts, but let's start with you doing Beth. Much less exciting, but then we can go on to Amy, which will be lots more fun."

"But I—" Lily started to explain that she was more interested in Beth anyway. Her mother wasn't listening.

"Oh, I know, but you do need to be prepared for both parts. Don't worry – we won't spend that long on this one." Lily's mum beamed at her. "I'll start, shall I?" And she launched into the scene. She *was* very good, Lily had to admit. She had subtly different voices for each of the girls and even her face seemed to transform when she changed character. Lily couldn't help remembering all the times her mum had acted out stories for her at bedtime – she had thought she was so lucky to have such a brilliant storyteller all to herself.

Grudgingly, she started to read Beth's lines and as the scene went on, some of her grumpiness melted away. She began to get a feel for it again – Beth's fear fighting with her need to be strong for her family. She felt quite pleased with herself as the scene ended.

"Hmmm." Her mother looked at her thoughtfully. "Ye-es. I think you're trying to do too much with it, darling. It's a very straight part. There's not really much point in trying to bring out something that isn't there."

Lily felt so hurt. However much she complained about her mum, she knew that she was a good actress and she desperately wanted her to be impressed. How could she say that Lily's reading of the part was all wrong? Had she messed it up completely? Mr. Lessing had really liked the way she tried to give Beth's lines a deeper meaning.

They went through the scene again and

this time Lily just said the lines as they were written, no frills. Beth was brave and saintly and that was it. Lily couldn't summon up much enthusiasm for it though – if that was how her mum thought the part should be done, she could see why she reckoned Amy was the better role.

"That's much more like it. Now, let's do Amy."

Reluctantly, Lily turned back to the beginning of the scene. What would her mum's take on Amy be? She couldn't help reading the scene unenthusiastically – she didn't even want to do this part! (Well, obviously, if they offered it to her she wouldn't actually say no…)

"Come on, Lily, put some life into it!" her mum said crossly, interrupting her in the middle of a line. "You're just not bothering!"

Lily started again, this time making a bit

more effort – she could tell her mother wasn't going to let her get away with anything less. But the thought of a whole weekend of this was torture. Her mum was obviously much more interested in this part. She kept breaking in with little comments and suggestions, most of which Lily agreed with and she could tell they were helping. When her mum read Amy's lines to show her what she meant, it was amazing – her thirty-five-year-old mum became the spoiled eleven-year-old. She just wished her mum was putting in all that effort for Beth's lines instead of Amy's.

After about the fifth read-through, she tried suggesting it. "Can we go back and look at Beth now?"

"Oh, I don't think we need to, darling. You were fine with those lines. Let's concentrate on the part you actually want."

Lily snapped. Her mum was taking over

again. Lily wasn't her clone! Why couldn't she listen to what Lily was saying? She jumped up. "Beth is the part I want, Mum! She's brilliant!"

Her mother looked confused. "Lily, that's just nonsense, anyone can see—"

"No, anyone can't! I really want to be cast as Beth and if you won't help me, that's fine. I'll do it on my own, *my* way!" And Lily walked out, ignoring her mum shouting after her.

Lily called up one of her friends from her old school who she'd kept in touch with and arranged to go and see a film with her. She wanted to be well out of the way for as much of the day as possible. A showdown with her mum was bound to happen, but she needed to put it off until she'd calmed down.

She got back home in time for dinner and a full family conference. Luckily her dad didn't seem to have decided whose side he was on. He was annoyed with Lily for walking out, even though she'd texted him to say where she was going. He had a real go at her about being responsible. Lily thought that remembering to text in the mood she'd been in was as much as they could expect, but she wisely decided not to say this.

"I had my phone," she put in, when her dad

stopped for breath at one point. "And I often go to the cinema with Molly on the weekend. I don't see why you're so worried about it."

Unfortunately, this set her dad going on his irresponsibly-dashing-off-without-permission thing again, so Lily tried a different tack. "Look, I'm sorry, but I was upset and I wanted to get out of the house. I couldn't ask Mum because it was her I was upset with!"

"Exactly!" her mother snapped. "You knew I would say no, so you just went anyway!"

"What were you so upset about?" her dad asked.

Lily stared at the table. How should she put this? She didn't want to sound whingy about it – her dad hated that. "Me and Mum don't agree about my audition scene. I want to do it differently – and my drama teacher agreed with what I was doing before! He thought I was doing Beth really well!" Lily forgot she was meant to be explaining to her dad, and left him looking confused while she tried to make her mum see. "I know you think it's a boring part, but I don't, and it's got to be up to me, hasn't it?" she asked pleadingly. She *so* wanted her mum to understand.

"So you basically don't want my help at all?" her mum said frostily.

"No, I don't mean that—"

"I would have thought, Lily, that you'd have the sense to make the most of your advantages." Her mother got up and stalked out. "But obviously not. Do it your way." Her voice was the haughty tone she'd used for a high society lady in a film once – it seemed to come over her whenever she was hurt and angry.

Lily gazed after her, her eyes filling with tears.

CHAPTER SIX
Lily's Secret

Lily and her mum didn't talk for the rest of the weekend. Lily stayed in her room most of the time. Her dad said he could see her point, but he wasn't going to interfere – it was up to Lily and her mum to sort it out between them. By Monday, Lily was desperate to get back to school and escape the atmosphere. But that morning, another bombshell hit.

She was sitting on the stairs, sorting her stuff into her bag – being at Shine meant having three different sets of dance clothes to wash and the staff got very snappy if you forgot bits of it. Hunting for her ballet tights, Lily suddenly tuned in to the conversation she'd been vaguely hearing from the kitchen.

"I don't think that's a very good idea." Her dad's voice.

"Why on earth not?" her mum said, sounding irritable. "I'm sure Julia wouldn't mind. I'd do the same for her."

"That's not the point, Marina! You're right – Julia would probably be quite happy to put in a good word for Lily with the director, but

Lily would hate that!"

"Lily is behaving like a spoiled child over this whole thing!" her mum snapped. "She needs to learn to make use of her connections and stop being so silly about it."

"Well, you're not even sure if Julia's been cast, so it doesn't matter." Her dad sighed. "I just think that you should leave Lily alone to get on with it. Interfering didn't really help before, did it?"

Lily listened, her heart thudding. Wild thoughts of running away and starting a new life rushed through her head. She wanted to be somewhere a very long way away where no one had ever heard of her mother. She was never going to get a chance to do this for herself!

"Mmm." It was a noncommittal murmur. Lily got the feeling her mum wasn't really listening to what her dad was saying. "I'll keep thinking."

Lily shoved the rest of her stuff into her bag – she no longer cared if she got told off for having the wrong tights – and stomped down the rest of the stairs very obviously, so they'd know she was coming and stop talking about her. Luckily, eating her breakfast while silently staring into space was normal for Lily, so no one commented, and she disappeared to school as soon as she reasonably could. She just wished she didn't have to go back home that night.

★★★

Lily arrived at school feeling exhausted. So much for weekends being restful! It would be so much better if she could talk to someone about all this – well, preferably three someones.

She knew her friends would be sympathetic and it would be good to get their different points of view. Bethany was sensible and helpful so she'd be reassuring, and Sara was really strong willed and she had her own mum problems. Chloe was doing the audition too, so it would be good to see what she thought about Lily's mum's coaching. But it was just too embarrassing! Lily wasn't the sort of person who off-loaded all her problems onto her friends. She was quite reserved, and she just couldn't imagine walking into class and telling them all that her mother was driving her crazy – and had been for the last seven years.

Lily had made friends with Bethany, Sara and Chloe because of a moment of openness after Lizabeth's cruel bullying, but it didn't mean she told them *everything*. And besides, if she spilled the whole story, she would feel so silly. Chloe had been to loads of professional castings for modeling and ads, and Sara had faced a grueling audition for her brilliant part in *Mary Poppins*. Lily's history with auditions was not so good…

Still glumly trying to work out whether stewing over it on her own was better than totally humiliating herself, Lily went to find Mr. Lessing for her coaching session. She was really hoping that concentrating on work would help her snap out of it.

Unfortunately, it was the other way around. Despite Mr. Lessing's helpful comments, Lily just couldn't get her mother's voice out of her mind. She totally lost her way in Beth's lines as she desperately tried to claw back the extra feeling she'd been putting into them originally. After ten minutes of struggling she was almost in tears. Mr. Lessing would think she just hadn't bothered! He'd think he'd been right after all and she wouldn't be allowed to do the audition!

Luckily, he didn't seem to see it that way.
"Did you work on it really hard over the
weekend?" he asked sympathetically.

"Mmm," Lily sniffed.

"You've probably just overdone it. Try to
relax – it'll come back. You really were doing
it brilliantly on Friday, Lily, you've just let
yourself get stressed. Now, the audition's after
school tomorrow. Don't panic!" He grinned
at her horrified face. "It's loads of time. We'll

work on it again tomorrow morning – maybe you need to forget about *Little Women* today and come to it fresh, OK?"

Mr. Lessing seemed really calm, but Lily couldn't help feeling that he must be staring worriedly after her as she headed for the door. If she was no good tomorrow either, would they stop her doing the audition? No one would want her showing up the school.

When she got to the Year Seven form room, the others were there already. Sara was telling Chloe and Bethany about her weekend of rehearsals. It sounded amazing.

"Did you meet all the rest of the cast?" Bethany asked.

"Yes, they were really nice to us. We met the other Jane and Michael as well. I'm so glad I'm acting with Nathan – I didn't like the other boy at all!"

"There's a surprise!" Chloe giggled.

Sara gave her a look and then she giggled too.

"OK, I know, maybe I am just a teensy bit biased."

"Has he actually asked you out yet?" Lily asked interestedly, dumping her bag and sitting on one of the tables. She was relieved to have something else to think about and this was good gossip.

"No." Sara bit her lip thoughtfully. "I think he would if we weren't seeing each other so often at rehearsals though. You see what I mean? Anyway, it's probably not a good idea at the moment – we need to get our heads around what we're doing. It's just nice having someone I really like around, that's all." She blushed slightly.

"How can you be so sensible?" Chloe wailed.

Sara grinned. "And I don't fancy telling my mum either!"

Lily almost flinched – so far the conversation had been mercifully mum-free.

"So how was everyone else's weekend?" Sara asked, smiling happily to herself.

"Oh, OK," Bethany said. "Didn't do much really. I went with my sister to one of her band rehearsals, that's all."

"I spent the whole weekend going over that script," Chloe said, serious for once. "I reckon I know the lines now, but it's difficult that we're auditioning for Amy *and* Beth – I'm worried I'm going to say the wrong ones."

"I don't think you will once you're feeling in character," Lily said. "I know what you mean though."

"Do you reckon you know the lines?" Chloe asked. "We could go over it together at break. Hey, I forgot to ask, how was your session with Mr. Lessing? Mine's not till lunch."

Lily shrugged. "It was all right." Again, something inside was pushing her to tell them everything, but she couldn't quite do it.

Bethany grinned. "I bet you don't need Mr. Lessing anyway – you've got your mum to help. You're so lucky. Hey, Chloe, I think you should complain. Lily's got an unfair advantage!" Bethany was only kidding and, really, Lily knew that. But after her nightmare weekend, and the terrible coaching session, the teasing was just too much.

"*Lucky!*" she snarled, jumping up. "Are you

out of your mind? I would have thought that my so-called friend would actually have a clue about what it was like…" She tailed off, realizing that the others were staring at her as though she'd just sprouted horns. She looked down, her eyes filling with tears. Apart from the first day of term, the others had never really seen her being anything but laid-back – maybe the horns would have been less of a shock.

"Hey!" Lily flinched as Bethany got up too, expecting her friend to have a go at her. But Bethany put an arm around her shoulders. "That was meant to be a joke – I mean, obviously it was a rubbish one. I'm really sorry, Lils. I wasn't trying to get at you. Hey, don't cry!" She looked anxiously at the other two, who were still staring at Lily in amazement.

"Sorry," Lily muttered, trying desperately to sniff back her tears.

"Not good enough." Sara's voice was gentle but decided. "You can't go off like that and then not tell us what's going on. Talk." She patted the table beside her. "Come on, sit down, both of you."

Guided by Bethany, Lily perched herself on the table again and the other three drew close around her. It felt nice being looked after like this. She looked around at their worried faces and realized that she'd been silly. If she'd told them about everything ages ago, she'd have been saved so much stress.

"My coaching session with Mr. Lessing was awful," she admitted. "I've got this horrible feeling he's going to withdraw me from the audition. And it's all my mum's fault," she added bitterly.

"How come?" Sara asked sympathetically.

"She spent ages making me work on the scene with her over the weekend. She's got a totally different take on it and it's so confusing! Now I feel like I don't have a clue. It's like she just wants me to do it her way and it doesn't matter what anyone else thinks." Her shoulders slumped. "It's the same with everything. She's always done this. Ever since—" She paused. Oh, who cared if she sounded babyish? She had to off-load. "You see, I've only ever had one professional audition—"

"Hey, I thought you said you'd never

auditioned for anything?" Chloe interrupted.

"Yeah, I know. That wasn't true." Lily gazed at the floor. No one said anything, but the curious silence deepened. She glanced up. All three of them were watching her intently.

"Go on," Bethany prompted, squeezing her shoulders.

And so Lily told them.

★★★

She had been five when she had her first audition – her mum would have started her much younger, but her dad thought she needed to understand more of what was going on before she started working. Mum and Dad were both at work that day, so Lily went to the audition with her *au pair*. She was used to her parents not being around though, and she really liked Celeste. Lots more than some of the other *au pairs* she'd had.

Even though Lily's mum had to go to work (a murder mystery series), she made a big fuss of her at breakfast, calling her a little star and telling her how exciting the day would be. Lily couldn't wait. From everything her mum had said she had expected to be treated like a princess at the audition, so it was a big shock when there were loads of other little girls there and no one was much interested in her.

She didn't get the part and she was gutted when she overheard one of the directors saying something about her being nothing like her mother. She came home in tears and didn't stop crying until her mum got home from her shoot. Celeste couldn't get her to go to bed and so she was sitting on the stairs in her Minnie Mouse pajamas, still crying, when her mum finally walked in.

Marina Ferrars was disappointed too, but she couldn't understand why Lily was so upset

– everyone got rejected. When Lily's dad got home, he found them both crying. Sitting on the stairs, with Lily sobbing into his office suit and his wife pacing up and down the hall, he tried to work out what was going on. Eventually, he managed to get the story of the day out of Lily, who'd practically lost her voice from crying. His five-year-old daughter told him that she was useless – and she never wanted to go to another audition again.

And that was it. Lily kept doing her classes and she shone in the shows her drama teacher organized, but even though her mum found loads of parts for her, Lily refused to try again. Even when Marina Ferrars got her daughter a walk-on part in a film that she was in herself, Lily wouldn't do it. Eventually her mum gave up trying to get Lily to audition again, but she was still determined that Lily was going to stage school when she was old enough. And what Lily's mum wanted, she tended to get.

★★★

Lily stopped and sighed. Maybe she'd made herself sound like a whiny baby, but she felt better anyway. Like she'd finally managed to take off some horrible grimy old clothes. She looked around at the others, hoping not to see any amused little smiles, but they just looked sympathetic.

"And that's why your mum made such a fuss about you getting in here, sending that letter and everything?" Bethany mused. Then she added, "Lily, has all of this got something to do with you asking Mr. Lessing for the audition in the first place? That did seem a bit weird."

Lily nodded. "Yeah. I didn't tell you what he actually said – I was too ashamed." It felt good to be admitting it finally. "He said why should he give me the chance when I'd not bothered all term – he was right. I'd been deliberately not trying." She glanced up at the others, who looked as shocked as she expected. "My mum kind of tricked me into auditioning for a place here. It's complicated." She sighed and explained about the bargain with her dad.

"And then she sent the letter, Bethany, like you said. It seemed as if the whole thing was nothing to do with me after all."

"Yeah, and we said then that there was no way it made any difference!" Sara burst out.

"My mum really thinks it did." Lily shrugged. "I don't know. I was just so angry. I was going to stay for a year like I promised and then go somewhere else. But things turned out differently. I mean…" She flushed. "I met all of you, and everyone's so dedicated and the classes are so good. I felt silly, like I was missing this big opportunity because I was in some pathetic sulk. And then when this part came along, I just couldn't pretend it didn't matter anymore." Tears trickled down her face. "And now my mum's stuffed it up again."

A sudden beeping noise interrupted her and she took her phone out of her pocket to read the text.

"Oh, no!" Lily laughed miserably. "Guess who this is from. 'Lily, find out audition date so I can arrange to come with you.' She can't even let me go to the audition on my own! Well, I suppose it doesn't matter. At this rate there's not even going to be an audition."

Sara, Bethany and Chloe looked at each other rather helplessly. They were automatically murmuring soothing nothings about it all being fine, but Lily was right. She wouldn't be allowed to do the audition if Mr. Lessing thought she wasn't good enough. And even if she did, there was no way she'd get the part if she was this stressed out!

"It'll be OK, I'm sure it will," Bethany said. "Look, Sara, you take Lily down to the bathrooms so she can wash her face. It'll be registration in a minute. You can't sit through the morning looking like that, can you?" She was giving Sara a "do as you're told, I've got a plan" look. Sara raised her eyebrows but shepherded Lily out anyway.

As soon as they'd gone, Bethany turned to Chloe. "Did you say you had your coaching session at lunch?"

"Yes?" Chloe sounded unsure why Bethany wanted to know.

"Well, do you mind if I come too? Just for a couple of minutes? I think we need to tell Mr. Lessing what's going on. He might be able to help. He at least ought to know why Lily's in such a state. It's so unfair. She's obviously got the worst history with auditions. It would be awful if this one got messed up too."

"I suppose so," Chloe said thoughtfully. "Do you think Lily'll be OK with that though? She's really private about this thing with her mum. She had a hard time even telling us."

Bethany made a face. "No, I think she'd hate it. Which is why I sent her off with Sara and why we're not going to tell her until we've done it."

"Ohhh." Chloe nibbled her thumbnail. "Um, OK."

"Don't worry, I'll do it," Bethany said quickly. "I was the one who made that silly comment about her mum."

"Mmm – that didn't really make any difference though. It just got her so cross she told us. And I think you're right. I'm just worried she's not going to like it."

"It can't be worse than missing the audition.

Mr. Lessing must be able to do something," Bethany said hopefully.

Bethany whispered her plan to Sara while they were supposed to be drawing map symbols in geography, and she agreed to distract Lily at lunch while Bethany sneaked off with Chloe. So now they just had to make Mr. Lessing understand.

He seemed rather surprised to see Bethany as well as Chloe when they walked nervously into the drama studio, but all he did was raise his eyebrows at them.

"Er, Bethany wants to ask you something," Chloe muttered.

Bethany gave her a "thanks very much" glare and then gave the drama teacher her sweetest smile. "We're a bit worried about Lily," she started, hoping he might break in and say that he was too. But his eyebrows just went up fractionally farther.

"You probably noticed she wasn't very good this morning," Bethany struggled on.

Mr. Lessing now proved himself to be one of those people who can raise one eyebrow higher than the other.

Bethany glared at him – he could be a bit more helpful. "Her mum is an actress and she spent all weekend making her rehearse the scene, and she wanted Lily to do it differently from how you wanted, and now Lily's all confused and stressed," she said. Mr. Lessing was looking a bit more sympathetic now, so she added, "Can't you do something about it? Her mum even wants to go to the audition with her!"

The eyebrows again.

At this point Chloe decided she ought to join in. "She's very, very good as Beth. It would be awful if she messed up the audition."

"Couldn't you talk to Lily's mum?" Bethany asked hopefully.

This time Mr. Lessing actually got as far as speaking. "How do you think Lily would feel about that?"

"She'd hate it, but she really wants this

part. She's got a – a feeling about it." Bethany sighed helplessly. She could tell they were sounding ridiculous. "Don't worry, it was a silly idea. Sorry. Sorry to have interrupted." She headed for the door.

"Hang on, Bethany." Mr. Lessing's voice had gotten about fifty degrees warmer. "That wasn't a no. I was considering giving Lily's parents a call anyway to see what was wrong."

"Oh." Bethany wondered why in that case he hadn't been more helpful, but she decided not to say so. "When are you going to phone them?" she asked instead.

"Let's put it this way," purred Mr. Lessing. "The sooner I get this coaching started, the sooner I get to a phone."

"Oh, right!" Bethany blushed scarlet and left in a hurry, leaving Chloe staring after her.

Bethany, Sara and Chloe spent the afternoon feeling very jittery – especially as they had no idea what to expect. Luckily, Lily was still too upset to notice. When Ms. Purcell's secretary interrupted their singing lesson to ask Lily to come to the office, they couldn't help exchanging meaningful glances. But Lily looked stricken.

"They're going to tell me I can't do the audition," she said in a heartbroken whisper.

"I bet they're not." Bethany gave her a little push toward the door. "Go on!"

Sure enough, Lily came back to singing ten minutes later, looking confused but happy. It was a pity that Mr. Harvey wasn't the kind of teacher who'd ever let you get away with private conversations in his class. He was cross enough about being interrupted as it was. So the girls had to wait until the end of school to interrogate her.

"What happened?" Bethany demanded as soon as Mr. Harvey had stalked out.

Lily shook her head, looking bewildered. "Ms. Purcell wanted to tell me that she'd spoken to my mum. Mr. Lessing was worried about me this morning, so they called her and they had this long talk about how the school prefers parents not to go to auditions if at all possible. And Ms. Purcell managed to convince her that it's better if she doesn't coach me because I shouldn't have too many influences, and they think I might have been overstressed. I don't know how she did it. Or how Mr. Lessing knew what was wrong."

Chloe was grinning manically and Sara kicked her. But unfortunately not before Lily noticed. She glanced quickly around at her three friends. "Did you tell him?" she asked slowly.

Bethany nodded apologetically. Somehow

admitting this was much worse than she'd
imagined, with Lily's dark eyes blazing at her.

Lily gasped. She looked furious, her face
incredibly white. She seemed not to be able
to breathe, and Bethany looked worriedly
at Sara and Chloe. She had a feeling she'd
made a horrible mistake. Lily's fingers were
clenched into her palms, her nails digging
in. Suddenly she launched
herself at Bethany,
as though she was
going to claw at
her face. But all
she did was hug
her.

"Thank you,
thank you,
thank you!"

CHAPTER SEVEN
The Audition

Bethany gasped with relief. "I thought for a minute you were going to strangle me!" she said, only half laughing. "I'm really sorry, Lily, we should have asked you, but, well, we thought you'd say no, and somebody had to do *something*."

Lily nodded, her face still pale. "And I'd never have told him. Oh, Bethany, I'm so glad you said that thing about my mum helping me out. If I'd never told you what was going on…"

She paused, looking thoughtful. "I've still got to go home and see what kind of a state my mum's in though."

"Do you think she'll be upset?" Chloe asked. She got on really well with her mum and she couldn't imagine having this sort of thing going on between them.

"I don't know. I guess so – I suppose it depends what Ms. Purcell actually said."

"She managed to sort *my* parents out," Sara said encouragingly. "And she did it perfectly, going on about the benefits of life experiences and one-to-one teaching. She had my mum totally convinced. Mum thinks Ms. Purcell's brilliant now."

"Maybe she'll manage another miracle then." Lily grinned. "Well, I don't have to worry about that till I get home. Anyone fancy going to that new juice bar around the corner? My treat – you all deserve it."

★★★

One raspberry smoothie later, Lily had to face going home. She knew her mum wasn't working that day, so she'd almost certainly be there. She opened the front door quietly, hoping not to be noticed.

"Darling!" Her mother swooped down on her, looking dreadful. She'd definitely been crying. Lily could tell from the puffiness around her eyes. "Why didn't you tell me I was putting too much pressure on you? I feel awful!"

Lily felt like saying, "Wasn't it obvious?" but decided it would be mean. "I didn't want to upset you – you were trying to help. It was hard to explain." Looking at her mum's concerned face, Lily suddenly felt much less resentful. She had only been trying to do her best for Lily, after all.

"You do understand that, don't you? I went about it the wrong way, but that is all I was trying to do."

Lily nodded slowly. She was almost disappointed that her mum wasn't cross. Lily had been planning how their argument would go and now she couldn't force herself to say what she really felt – that her mother had been trying to mold her into a mini version of herself. For a moment they'd nearly been at the point where they could have it all out, but Lily just wasn't brave enough to go there if she didn't have to.

"Your principal said you need to take it really easy tonight, darling. No looking at the audition piece, going to bed early, all of that. Have you got more coaching tomorrow?" Then she flinched as she heard herself say this. "You don't have to tell me!" she backtracked quickly.

Lily was torn between laughing and crying. What on earth had Ms. Purcell done to her mother? Lily wasn't sure she wouldn't prefer the original version back.

"It's OK," she said. "I've got another session before school tomorrow. Then the audition's in the afternoon. I'd better go and do my homework," she muttered, desperate to get away. This was awful!

Her mother nodded and gazed after her as she ran up the stairs to her room. Lily felt like crying – her mother had been as nice about it as she possibly could have been, and it had been like talking to a total stranger.

She couldn't even talk to her dad as he was working late. But one thing was for certain. After what Bethany and the others had done for her today, there was no way she could mess up the audition, however weird everything was. She was going to go in there and do it her way. If that wasn't what the casting team wanted, then fine. But she would have tried.

★★★

"Oh, I'm so nervous! This is so exciting!" Chloe couldn't stop giggling as the school chaperone signed them all in at the front desk.

The TV production company that was making *Little Women* was in a very smart building a short ride from Shine and they'd been sent over straight after school. The two Year Eight girls were trying to look as though they'd done this millions of times before and kept giving them looks, but Chloe, Lily, Emily and Lauren didn't care.

"You've done lots of auditions before!" Lauren said. "You've even been in a TV series, Chloe, how can you be nervous?"

"I know, but I still am!"

They were being shepherded toward a very plush elevator and Lily's heart began to thump. She was trying so hard not to think of that previous audition disaster, and she was clutching the script so tightly that her fingers had gone white.

Because the audition had been arranged through the school, it was only the six of them there. The schedule was tight – there would be girls from other theatre schools following their slot and apparently the producers were intending to make a decision that afternoon. It seemed crazy to Lily that she would have ten minutes at the most to convince these people she was right for the part. A thought suddenly struck her – her mum must have done this thousands of times.

Everyone in the production company offices seemed to be rushing around and the girls stood nervously, watching as they got signed in yet again. The atmosphere reminded Lily of her other audition – the way no one actually seemed that interested in them.

They were swept off to wait in a tiny room, and Lily was horrified when the girl in charge told her that she was going first. Still, at least it would get it over with. She gave Chloe a slightly panicked smile, and then followed the girl into another room.

A man and a woman were sitting at a table covered with photographs. Lily realized that the school must have sent her photo over too. In fact, the man was holding it and looking at her as though he was making sure it was definitely the same person. Lily suddenly wished it was a nicer picture – it had been taken to go with her application form for the school and she'd been really sulky. Not at all Beth-like.

"This is Lily. She's the first of the girls from Shine," said the girl who'd brought her in. "Lily, this is Jackson, he's the producer, and Annie, the casting director. I'm Annie's assistant, Meera, and I'll be reading the other parts for the audition. OK?"

Lily nodded, worrying that her voice might do something weird if she tried to say yes.

"Just stand over there, Lily," said the casting director, smiling. She murmured something to the producer, which Lily thought sounded like, "Perfect look, don't you think?" and he nodded. It could have been loads of other things, but it made Lily feel slightly better. She was fifty percent sure that she'd actually be able to speak when she tried now.

"Let's start with you as Beth, Lily," the casting director continued.

Lily opened the script. She was pretty sure she didn't need it, but having something to hold was making her feel more confident.

As Meera started to speak Meg's familiar words, Lily relaxed. Her practice with Mr. Lessing that morning had been really good – she felt like she knew Beth again and she wanted everyone else to know her too, to see how brave she was, how desperate that Amy shouldn't catch the fever from her. She forgot about worrying where her voice had gone and just spoke.

Meera smiled at her when she finished and Lily blinked awkwardly. For a few minutes she hadn't felt as though she was in an office building in the middle of London at all. She looked anxiously at the casting director and producer, and saw that they were smiling too.

"And now let's hear you as Amy," said the casting director, scribbling notes.

Lily tried to put the same effort in, but she could tell that although she was reading the part well, the same spark wasn't there. She couldn't help feeling that this was Chloe's part anyway…

"Thank you, Lily. Can you stand over there, so we can take a few more photos of you?"

Meera grabbed a digital camera from the table, and Lily tried to look relaxed and not at all sulky. She had no idea what someone nearly dying of scarlet fever looked like, so she just hoped she looked a bit fragile. She *felt* fragile.

And then she was outside.

★★★

Lily didn't know how to feel as she walked home from the station. It was hard to believe the audition was over. She'd only known that the part of Beth existed for a week, but it seemed as if she'd been aiming toward this afternoon for years. Now that it was over, she felt completely limp. Ms. Shaw was going to call later on with news, but Lily was almost too tired to care.

Lily's mum was reading a script at the kitchen table and Lily slumped down opposite her. Her mum looked at her with her head on one side. "Do you fancy a bacon sandwich?" she asked.

Lily laughed weakly. It really wasn't the question she'd been expecting, but actually, yes, a bacon sandwich would be perfect.

"You look shattered," her mum said as she

slipped the bacon under the grill and sliced some bread.

"It's ridiculous," Lily replied. "The audition only took ten minutes, but I feel like I've been running a marathon or something."

"Mmm."

Lily sighed. Her mother was so obviously trying not to say anything that might upset her. The thing was, she was quite used to her mum chatting away about auditions and that kind of thing. Supertactful mother just seemed wrong.

"I thought of you as I was about to go into the audition," she said suddenly.

Her mother turned around from the grill, looking hopeful and scared all at once. "I just realized that you must have waited outside thousands of auditions," Lily explained. "That smells really good," she added.

"I always have to have a bacon sandwich

afterward," her mum said, sliding the plate over to her. "The nerves make me feel so hungry." She grinned and bit into her own sandwich. "I've never been as nervous as today though. I don't think I've actually read my script at all – or if I have it's really terrible because I can't remember a word of it."

"You were nervous because I was doing an audition?" Lily asked curiously.

"Mmm. Especially after what your teachers said. I didn't realize what I was doing, Lily, you do know that? And I am really sorry."

Lily, looking thoughtful, put ketchup on her sandwich. "It felt like you wouldn't let me do anything for myself." She looked up at her mum challengingly, daring her to deny it.

But her mum was nodding. "Absolutely."

Lily stared at her. How could she just sit there and agree?

"Lily, I didn't want you to have to! It's been

so difficult sometimes. I was trying to use my
experience to protect you. But I can't – you
have to do it for yourself. I just hope I haven't
spoiled this audition for you."

Lily shook her head slowly. "I don't think so
– it seemed to go OK. Oh. I don't know!"

Her mum shrugged. "I can never tell either,"
she admitted. "Do you know when you'll
hear?"

Lily looked up at the clock. "Ms. Shaw's
going to phone us all if they let her know in

time. They're supposed to decide tonight. They want to get started on the filming over Christmas."

And with perfect dramatic timing, the phone started to ring.

Lily nearly knocked her plate off the table. She stared at her mum, her eyes round with panic.

"Answer it, darling," her mum said, trying to sound calm.

Lily shook her head. "No. You answer it for me. Please. I want you to." And she smiled. Suddenly it seemed like she and her mum actually had something in common. They were both terrified!

With shaking fingers, her mum reached for the phone.

"Hello? Yes, Marina Ferrars speaking. Oh. Oh right."

Lily stared at her mother, her heart

thudding. Her face was unreadable – well, she was an actress.

Suddenly her mother winked at her, and Lily's heart stopped thudding and jumped into her mouth instead. "I'll tell her. Thanks so much. Yes, goodbye!"

"What? What what what?" Lily squeaked.

"You got it! Oh, Lily, all by yourself! I'm so proud of you!"

Lily jumped at her, squeezing her tight in a huge hug. "You helped!"

And, despite everything, she knew it was true.

HOLLY WEBB

Holly Webb started out as a children's book editor and wrote her first series for the publisher she worked for. She has been writing ever since, with over one hundred books to her name. Holly lives in Berkshire, UK, with her husband and three young sons. Holly's pet cats are always nosying around when she is trying to type on her laptop.

For more information
about Holly Webb visit:

www.holly-webb.com